International Standard Book Number 1-55868-033-0
Library of Congress Catalog Number 90-71079
© MCMXC by Graphic Arts Center Publishing Company
P.O. Box 10306 • Portland, Oregon 97210 • 503-226-2402
President • Charles M. Hopkins
Editor-in-Chief • Douglas A. Pfeiffer
Managing Editor • Jean Andrews
Designer • Becky Gyes
Typographer • Harrison Typesetting, Inc.
Printer • Moore Lithograph, Inc.
Bindery • Lincoln & Allen
Printed in the United States of America

Nestled high on the top of a mountain
is a place called Timberline Lodge, where
there is shelter, good food, and love. But most
of all there is—and always will be—Heidi.

STEPHEN

Forests and trees do not grow on the highest of the highest mountains, and above where the forests grow is timberline. Here, in deference to this windswept magic, Nature refuses to let the mighty timbers stand. Here, even in the delight of springtime, the air is crystal clear and cool. One such mountain of higher than high looms far above a vast valley that is filled with people.

Built in the mountain's shadow and the icy fingers of the blue-light glaciers is a massive, wood-beamed inn called Timberline Lodge. Snows, long-since fallen, melt slowly, dripping down long, silver icicles, puddling in pools that overflow and fill tiny creeks, that fill bubbling brooks, that fill roaring rivers. The rivers flow to still larger rivers to continue Nature's race to the mighty Pacific Ocean.

Much like the mountain itself, Timberline Lodge exudes a sense of timelessness, a place that will always be. Here, seemingly out of place, stretched out in a shafted patch of warm, golden sunlight, is the biggest dog you will ever see—a great Saint Bernard. What you can't see, but can only sense, is her heart, which is nearly as big as the mountain itself. Her name is Heidi, and she has been here a long, long time, and it is forever she will be welcome here.

However, Heidi has not been at Timberline forever, and many, many years before, no one even knew her name.

It was springtime then, also a long time ago, a time of slowly melting snows. Here then, green, hardy shoots of mountain flowers-to-be forced their way through the frost and rime to drink the golden light of life. But there was discord here—something just not right and slightly wrong. That discord took form and substance in the shape of a very spoiled ten-year-old girl by the name of Rose McGilly. Rose lived here at the lodge alone with her widowed father who was the keeper of the inn, the manager, if you like.

It is sad not to have a mother; it is sadder still to have a father that never seems to understand. Just that morning Rose had cajoled and begged her father for her "latest" heart's desire. "Oh, Father," she cried, "I must have a puppy like the other kids at school. Please!"

"Listen, Rose," said her father firmly, "you want and you want, but you never seem to want to give of yourself. The chef says that you have been in the kitchen yelling at the staff to get you this and get you that. We all work here together, and that includes you." With that, he turned on his heel and started to leave the room.

"But, Daddy!" cried Rose. "What about my puppy?"

"No buts, young lady; you can have a puppy when you learn to care for others as much as you selfishly care for yourself."

As he left the room, Rose made a very ugly face at her father.

Several weeks later, as the days of spring stretched into the longer days of summer, Rose was in the kitchen bossing everyone about when she heard a scratching and a whining from the kitchen door. Her eyes opened wide, and she laughed, "It's my puppy. I knew Daddy wouldn't let me down. He never does."

She ran to the door, threw it open wide and dropped to her knees to hug her new pet. But there was no puppy to hug. Instead, there stood the biggest dog Rose had ever seen—a full-grown Saint Bernard. Before she could cry out, before she could even get to her feet, a tongue that seemed as long as the Columbia River, and nearly as wet, licked her from the tip of her chin all the way up her face in one big slurp.

"Oh, yuuuck!" groaned Rose, as she wiped her face with her sleeve.

Satisfied at the welcome, the huge dog thundered into the kitchen, as the staff laughed at Rose's plight. Not to be outdone by some upstart dog, Rose grabbed a broom and set after the bear-sized animal. With even the chef holding his sides in laughter, she chased after the dog, who was sitting quite contentedly near the sink.

Rose lifted the broom high into the air and would have struck the dog had she not noticed around the dog's neck a beautiful, ivory-colored locket with a single, long-stemmed rose etched on it. Rose carefully lowered the broom and reached to snatch the locket, but the dog bared her teeth and growled ominously. Rose retrieved her hand in fear that if she left it near the maw of this great beast it might be snapped off and munched down as if it were some treat. After all, the dog had just tasted her face.

By this time, the staff had begun to gather around, wondering and muttering about this mysterious dog.

"Whose dog is it?" someone asked.

And yet another, "The owner's name must be in the locket. I'll bet there's a reward."

"The only reward I want," snapped Rose, "is that locket!" With that, she reached her hand once again to grab the jewelry, but again, the dog was faster and growled a deep, frightening growl.

Just at that moment, Rose's father appeared and laughingly said, "Well, everyone is welcome at Timberline Lodge, and I guess that includes Saint Bernards. But if no one has claimed it or if no one has been able to look inside the locket, then I'll call the authorities so they can dispose of the dog."

Rose looked about as her father left the kitchen, a million plans to recover the locket racing through her devious mind.

It was not long before her eyes lit up as she devised a marvelous plan. Without so much as a "how do you do," she walked over to the meat cooler and removed a large steak. The chef tapped his foot, his eyes narrow and angry, but the girl shrugged casually and said, "It's just the steak I was going to have for dinner. I'll have vegetables instead." Rose rushed to the huge dog who was looking up at her with soulful eyes, her massive head resting on her paws. "Here, puppy. A nice piece of meat to make us friends." With that, she tossed the meat in the air. The dog looked up, opened her mouth, and closed it with a snap—and just like that the steak was gone. No muss, no burp, no bother.

Rose reached for the locket that was now surely hers. Her hand moved a little closer this time before the huge dog growled her ominous warning.

Shaking her head in disbelief, Rose ran from the kitchen and was back in but a flash with a bright yellow tennis ball. She held the ball teasingly above her head, "Come on, puppy, let's play!" And play they did, as Rose tossed that ball all afternoon long, and the dog happily chased and retrieved it. But no matter how hard the girl tried, the locket and the dog's friendship were quite unattainable.

Dinner that night was bizarre at best, for Rose had to eat an uninteresting meal of broccoli, spinach, and rutabagas, specially prepared by a glittering-eyed chef who watched through the open kitchen door as she choked down bite after bite and her father curiously looked on. Fortunately, she was able to snitch an extra lemon square from the dessert tray as she scampered up the steps from the dining room.

But now Rose was faced with a real dilemma: what to do with the dog while she was asleep. "I can't turn her loose," she said, as the dog stared at her with mournful eyes. "One of the staff is bound to wait until she falls asleep and then steal the locket. No, this puppy's spending the night with me!"

Rose lured the huge dog down to the family room of the inn with bits and pieces of her lemon square that was to have been relished and cherished later. Step by step and crumb by crumb, the dog followed. Once in her cheery room, Rose slammed the door, and the dog and locket were safe. One of the housekeepers had already turned down her bed and lit a crackling fire in the quaint little fireplace in her room. Assuming the dog would find its own place to sleep, she changed quickly into her nightgown and brushed her teeth the "quick-spit" way.

With her clothes left carelessly in a someone-else-will-pick-them-up heap, she turned off the bathroom light. In the dancing shadows of the fireplace flicker, she scampered to bed but was shocked to see that the dog had indeed found a place to sleep for the night . . . in the middle of Rose's bed! "What a bother," she grumbled resignedly. "Now I have to sleep with the elephant dog. Oh well, at least no one will be able to slip in during the night and steal my locket." With that, she started to climb into bed, but was frozen in place by the low, grumbling growl of the massive dog, who watched her warily from the middle of the bed.

Angry, but unable to do anything else, Rose pulled the extra quilt from the end of the bed, and, with spare pillow in hand, she curled up on the stone hearth. "Tomorrow," she mumbled as she tried to find a soft place on the old, weathered stones, "tomorrow the locket will be mine, and the dog can be off to the dog pound for all I care." From the bed, a comfy Saint Bernard sighed a great big sigh and fell fast asleep.

Many hours later as the dark of night was just changing into the steel-gray light of dawn, Rose woke with a start from her stone-hearth bed. She looked about the room and, in a flash, remembered all that had happened. But what had wakened her? Suddenly, the room rumbled, and even the pictures on the wall rattled in their frames. "Geez," she thought, "that dog even snores like an elephant." Her eyes opened wide as she realized that with the huge beast asleep she had her chance to grab the locket from around her neck. "This time I'm taking no chances," she thought as she slipped from under the quilt. "I'll tie the dog up before I take the locket."

With warm feet on the cold, wooden floor, she tip-toed to her closet, and there she found a small coil of rope she had used over time for one project or another. She took the rope carefully and quietly tied one end around the wrought-iron handle of the door. As the dog rumbled, deep in sleep, Rose slipped to the bed and carefully—oh, so carefully—tied the other end about the dog's great neck. Then she began to remove the locket. She had not pulled it more than halfway over the animal's head when the dog woke up, and the two were eye to eye. Rose jumped back; the dog jumped up and soon discovered that she was tied to the door. She struggled, clambering off the bed and making a terrible racket as she tossed her great head this way and that, trying to escape from the choking rope.

Rose just laughed at the dog. "You're mine now," she chuckled gleefully, "and so is the locket!"